We're Moving

Heather Maisner

ILLUSTRATED BY Kristina Stephenson

KINGFISHER

BOSTON

I don't want to move, Amy thought, looking
out of the window at the flowers she'd planted
with her dad and her best friend, Eve.

I'll miss Eve, and I'll miss the flowers.

Crash! Bang! Whack!

Behind her, Ben threw toy cars into a box, shouting, "We're off! We're off!" as he zoomed around the room.

"Time to go," said Mom.

The car was crowded. Figaro's cat box took up half the backseat. Eve ran up and thrust a blue, furry teddy bear into Amy's hands.

"Take this," she said. And she waved and waved as the car drove off.

Amy cuddled the blue bear. Ben sang. Figaro meowed, and Dad drove for miles and miles.

The new house echoed. Men walked in and out, carrying boxes. There were no pictures on the walls or curtains on the windows, and the furniture stood higgledy-piggledy in the middle of each room.

Ben ran up and down the stairs, shouting, "Here we are! Here we are!"

Amy stared out at the wild backyard,
thinking, *There aren't any flowers.*

That night Amy lay in bed, feeling scared and lonely.
In the old house she had shared a room with Ben.
The moon cast shadows through the window.
A door rattled. Pipes gurgled, and a car swooshed
past down the road. Amy shivered. Then she
heard a strange sniffling sound.

The floorboards creaked, and footsteps moved toward
her. She was about to scream when a little voice said,
"Can I come in your bed? I don't like it on my own."
"Oh, all right," said Amy.
Ben climbed in beside her, and Amy was secretly pleased.

The next day Mom
was busy emptying boxes.
Dad was balanced on a
chair, putting up a
lamp shade.

Ben couldn't find his favorite green toy car.

"I've left it behind," he wailed. "We have to go back."

"I'll help you look for it," said Amy.

Amy and Ben searched every room.
They found a dusty book in a cupboard . . .

a necklace under a carpet . . .

and two dirty socks
behind a radiator.

They crept downstairs to the cold, dark basement. They found an old boot and lots of scurrying spiders, but they couldn't find the green car anywhere.

"Let's try the yard," said Amy.

They made a path through the weeds to an overgrown pond. A frog jumped into the water with a plop. Birds fluttered and squawked. Figaro sat staring over the tall grass. Ben found a rope swing hanging from a tree, and Amy swung high up into the sky.

Splattered with mud, they
ran back into the house.
"Take off your shoes,"
Mom shouted as they
raced upstairs.

Amy's room looked completely different. It had
curtains and a rug, and all her teddy bears sat in a
row on the bed, just like they did in the old house.

Amy slid her feet into her slippers, but she couldn't get one on. She frowned and bent down. Ben's favorite green car was hiding inside.

"I've found it," she called. "I've found it."

The next day
they went shopping.
Amy chose pink
and purple paint
for her room.

Ben chose
wallpaper with
tractors all over it.

Mom bought everything in yellow for the kitchen.
Dad bought a drill and a new set of tools.
They walked back to the car with their packages.

Suddenly, Amy stopped in front of a garden center.
Dad bumped into her, almost dropping his packages.

"What is it?" he asked. "What's wrong?"

But Amy didn't answer. She couldn't. She bit her lip hard
to hold back the tears.

Dad looked over his mountain of packages and said,
"Oops, there's something we've forgotten."

He hurried into the store and came out with two trays of flowering plants, just like the ones they'd had at the old house.

"Thanks!" said Amy, jumping up to kiss him.

Later Dad and Amy worked in the yard.

A boy and a girl leaned over the fence to watch.

"What are you doing?" asked the boy.

"Planting flowers," said Amy.

"Can we help?" asked the girl.

Amy nodded, and they all dug holes in the ground while Dad mowed the lawn. Then they had a grass fight.

"I'm Lucy," said the girl. "And this is George."

"I'm Amy," said Amy. "Do you want to see our house?" And she ran inside with her new friends.

The publisher thanks Eileen Hayes, parenting adviser for the U.K. child protection charity NSPCC, for her kind assistance in the development of this book.

For Rosie and Ruby—H. M.
For Maddie and Charlie—K. S.

KINGFISHER
a Houghton Mifflin Company imprint
222 Berkeley Street
Boston, Massachusetts 02116
www.houghtonmifflinbooks.com

First published in 2004
2 4 6 8 10 9 7 5 3 1

LIBRARY OF CONGRESS CATALOGING-IN-PUBLICATION DATA
has been applied for.

ISBN 0-7534-5739-3

Printed in Singapore
1TR/0704/TWP/PICA(PICA)/150MA